First published 2018 by Walker Books Ltd
87 Vauxhall Walk, London SE11 5HJ

2 4 6 8 10 9 7 5 3 1

© 1986, 1993, 1994, 2018 Shirley Hughes

This book has been typeset in Sabon

Printed in China

British Library Cataloguing in Publication Data:
a catalogue record for this book is
available from the British Library

ISBN 978-1-4063-8171-9

www.walker.co.uk

MOTHER'S DAY

Shirley Hughes

WALKER BOOKS
AND SUBSIDIARIES
LONDON · BOSTON · SYDNEY · AUCKLAND

I love spending time
with my mum.

Sometimes Olly and I play
hide and seek with Mum when
she's trying to make the beds.

Mum isn't very good at hiding.

But Mum's keys are good at hiding, especially when we're all ready to go out.

When we go to the park,
Mum takes us to see
the fish in the pond.

Or if we go to the supermarket,
Mum gets cakes for tea.

We wait with Mum when
the light is red...

And then we walk with Mum
when the light is green.

Sometimes we run
as fast as we can…

Sometimes we stop to
look at interesting things.

We like it
when Mum
takes us on
the bus...

And when we get home,
Mum likes to
sit down for a bit.

Sometimes we help Mum
make the dinner...

And Mum helps us
have a bath.

Today, Mum had
a special day.

Today, I gave Mum
a little present and a card
I drew for her...

And she gave me
a cuddle and
a bedtime story.

I love spending time
with my mum.